PUFFIN BOOKS

Harry and Daphne and the Amazing Reversing Powder

Margaret Pinder lives in Yorkshire with her daughter, Freya, with whom she has been around the world three times. In the course of what she likes to call her career she has practised maritime law in London and corporate law in Manhattan, taught writing at Harvard University and worked as a translator. When she is not playing the double bass, studying South-East Asian drama, or writing, she tries to understand the Meaning of Life. She would like to assure her readers that no animals were harmed in the writing of this book.

For Freya

MARGARET PINDER

Harry and Daphne and the Amazing Reversing Powder

Illustrated by Kevin McAleenan

PUFFIN BOOKS

PUFFIN BOOKS

Published by the Penguin Group
Penguin Books Ltd, 80 Strand, London WC2R 0RL, England
Penguin Putnam Inc., 375 Hudson Street, New York, New York 10014, USA
Penguin Books Australia Ltd, 250 Camberwell Road, Camberwell, Victoria 3124, Australia
Penguin Books Canada Ltd, 10 Alcorn Avenue, Toronto, Ontario, Canada M4V 3B2
Penguin Books India (P) Ltd, 11 Community Centre, Panchsheel Park, New Delhi – 110 017, India
Penguin Books (NZ) Ltd, Cnr Rosedale and Airborne Roads, Albany, Auckland, New Zealand
Penguin Books (South Africa) (Pty) Ltd, 24 Sturdee Avenue, Rosebank 2196, South Africa

Penguin Books Ltd, Registered Offices: 80 Strand, London WC2R 0RL, England

www.penguin.com

First published 2000
4

Text copyright © Margaret Pinder, 2000
Illustrations copyright © Kevin McAleenan, 2000
All rights reserved

The moral right of the author and illustrator has been asserted

Made and printed in England by Clays Ltd, St Ives plc

British Library Cataloguing in Publication Data
A CIP catalogue record for this book is available from the British Library

ISBN 0–141–30715–3

Chapter One

People tell me crocodiles are by nature
untruthful, so you may find it hard to
believe what I am about to tell you. Not
because *I* am a crocodile, no. But I did
know two crocodiles once, Harry and
Daphne, and this is their story.

I remember the first time I saw them,
on the banks of the Heavy River, in the
heart of the Thickening Jungle. I had

searched all day and found nothing until, disheartened, I had sat down on the prominent roots of a Trembling Tree to rest. I could see the crocodiles, two of them, lying like old, rolling logs in the muddy waters, asleep.

Or were they?

As I opened my tin of Fortifying and Sustaining Snacks, I watched them idly. They were an impressive pair. The larger of the two was especially striking. Its dappled hide was criss-crossed with faint markings that looked almost like stitching.

It was then that I realized the crocodile was watching me. One dull, yellow eye had flicked open, closed and opened again. The crocodile had winked at me! Then it moved. It lifted its snout out of the water and looked

straight at me. I was glad I was safe in
the roots of the Trembling Tree, but I
could not help closing the lid of my tin
and holding it tightly.

Then the crocodile spoke.

'You're looking for the Snipers,' it
said. 'Aren't you?'

How can I describe the sound? The
voice of the crocodile is the voice of the

slow, muddy river itself. It is thick water sucking over old, dead trees. It is silt oozing over long-forgotten rocks. It is deep and dark and clouded.

Now the other crocodile joined in.

'Shh!' it whispered, and appeared to elbow the other in the side. 'Harry!'

The first crocodile sank a little deeper in the water, still staring at me. Surely my ears were deceiving me, but that steady, yellow gaze left me in no doubt. If the crocodile could wink, then surely it could speak.

'Yes,' I said. 'I am.'

'Well you won't find them,' the crocodile said. 'They're gone.'

At this, its friend elbowed it sharply once more.

'Harry, that's enough,' it hissed. 'You go getting yourself mixed up with humans again and we'll be back where we started. Come on. I'm off.'

With that, it twisted its great body in the water and began to swim away. The first crocodile looked, winked again, then turned and began to follow.

'Wait!' I cried, scrambling forward over the roots of the Trembling Tree. 'Come back! The Snipers! Where are they? Tell me, please!'

But the crocodiles neither stopped nor turned and I watched their muddy backs disappearing down the Heavy River. Only their voices drifted back to me.

'Lay off, Daphne. I was only trying to help. The poor bloke's been looking for days now.'

'I don't care. He's a human and humans is bad news. As if you didn't know. Only this time you needn't think I'd come after you again.'

'But you would, wouldn't you, Daph? You know you would. Now, cheer up and give us a kiss.'

'Oh stop it, Harry! Your breath!'

Then, with one last distant sound that was both a chuckle and a giggle, they were gone.

Chapter Two

I spent a restless night, the Thickening
Jungle booming and whispering all
around me, but as dawn broke through
the canopy of high leaves I fell into a
fitful doze. When I awoke, the sun was
bright on my face and … the crocodiles
were back!

For a few moments they stared hard
at me. Then the one called Harry lifted

his snout from the water and spoke again.

'Daphne and me have been having a confabulation,' he said. 'And we want to know exactly what you're doing here. Right, Daph?'

He turned his dark eyes towards the crocodile at his side.

'Yes,' she said. 'If you're anything to do with the Snipers we want to know.'

What could I say?

'I'm afraid in one way I am,' I stammered.

'I told you so, Harry,' said the second crocodile. 'Let's be off.'

'No! Please!' I cried. 'Let me explain.'

The first crocodile paused.

'Let's listen to what he has to say, love,' he said. His friend was already sinking below the water. 'Listening can't do any harm.'

'No harm at all!' I cried. 'I have been sent to find the truth. No more. And, if you can help me, I would be most grateful.'

Daphne, for I shall call them both by name now, looked at me warily.

'Are you sure?' she said heavily.

'Quite sure, my dear lady,' I reassured her.

My words seemed to impress her. She giggled and nudged Harry.

'Did you hear that?' she said. 'Oh my!'

'All right, Daphne,' said Harry a little impatiently. He addressed me again.

'First things first: do you have a gun?'

'No,' I said truthfully. 'I do not.'

The crocodiles seemed to consider this.

'I do not like them,' I went on. 'They frighten me.'

Harry grunted and nudged Daphne. I waited.

'Anything else like that then?'

'I have a knife,' I said. 'A machete, for clearing my way through the jungle.'

'Have you ever hurt or killed an animal with it?' (This was Daphne.)

'Never.'

'Would you?'

'Only in self-defence,' I said. 'Or maybe if I were hungry and needed food.'

'That's fair enough,' said Harry. 'All right then. What are you doing here and how do you know the Snipers?'

'I don't know them,' I said. 'I only know who they are. Or were,' I added, looking quickly at the crocodiles, but their faces gave nothing away. 'They used to live here, but nothing has been seen or heard of them for over three months. The British consul has sent me to find out what has happened.'

I sat down on the Trembling Tree and looked sadly at my poor scratched and blistered hands.

'It's not a job I'm suited to,' I said. 'I've only worked in an office until now,

reading papers, filing. Believe me, I
didn't want to come, but there was no
one else.'

'Poor thing,' said Daphne quietly.

'Yes, well,' said Harry, clearing his
impressive throat. 'So what will you do
if, and I say "if" not "when", you find
out?'

'I shall return and make my report,'
I said with dignity, although the
thought of my tidy little desk with its
neat piles of papers had brought tears
to my eyes.

'Oh yes?' said Harry. 'Then what?'

'Nothing,' I replied. 'Why?'

'So there'd be no more people
coming here,' said Daphne. 'No more
search parties. No more expeditions
looking for …'

'Revenge,' said Harry.

'Oh no, nothing of that kind,' I said quickly. 'If I find them …'

But Harry interrupted.

'No worries then, Daphne, eh?'

He sounded almost cheerful.

'Please,' I said. 'If you know anything, if you can help me, I beg you, please do.'

'Well,' said Daphne, 'Harry and I

decided last night if you sounded OK, we would.'

'That's right,' said Harry. 'And you seem a decent bloke, so we'll tell you what we know.'

'One moment,' I said, fumbling in my pocket. 'My pencil! My notebook!'

'You won't need them,' said Harry. 'If you can turn our story into a nice tidy report for your consul, you can turn me back into a handbag, and welcome!'

He chuckled, deep in his chest.

'He's right,' said Daphne gently. 'You'd better just listen. Go on, Harry, you start.'

My head still spinning, I settled myself back against the trunk of the Trembling Tree and listened.

Harry cleared his throat majestically. A silence seemed to fall over the

Heavy River.

'What you have to understand,' he began solemnly, 'is what the Snipers were really like ...'

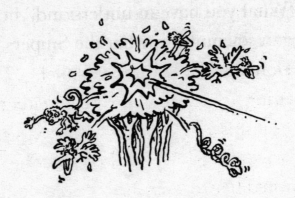

Chapter Three

BANG!
BANG!

There was a thin, high scream from the leaves and the thud of something falling into the undergrowth.

'If it moves, shoot it!' said Colonel Sniper, lowering his rifle and leaning it against the breakfast table. 'Eh what?'

'Absolutely, darling,' said Lady Sniper,

taking her hands from over her ears and helping herself to another slice of bacon. 'What was it?'

'Don't know,' said the Colonel, spearing a sausage. 'Don't care either. Does it matter?'

'No, darling,' his wife replied. She adjusted her tortoiseshell glasses on her long, thin nose and peered across the lawn. 'I just wondered.'

An animal had appeared on the far side of the lumpy grass that surrounded the house and was waddling towards the veranda. It was a dog: a large, squat, ugly dog. The Colonel reached for his gun.

'No, darling,' said Lady Sniper quickly. 'It's only Wattles.'

The Colonel grunted and picked up his knife and fork again.

'He's got something. Probably
whatever it was you shot. Coo-ee,
Wattles! Come to Mumsy!' called Lady
Sniper, flapping her hands.

The dog quickened its pace and
disappeared round the side of the
house. Lady Sniper sat down and began
to pout.

'There, there, my little forest lily,' said the Colonel. 'Cheer up. We're going hunting for something bigger and better than that today.'

Lady Sniper brightened. She leaned forward eagerly. Some of her hair escaped from the untidy pile on the top of her head and flopped over her ear, scattering pins on the table. Her bone-bead necklace clattered into her coffee cup.

'We are?' She clapped her bony hands together. 'Oh, what will it be today? Do tell!'

'Don't know myself yet,' said the Colonel smugly. 'But there are still a few gaps on the wall in there.' He jerked his head back towards the house. 'Always room for more, I say.'

He pretended to lift his gun and point it at his wife. 'Bang! Bang!' he said cheerfully.

Lady Sniper gave a little scream of delight.

'Lovely! Lovely!' she cried.

The Colonel began to sing in a cracked baritone.

Oh a-hunting we will go.

A-hunting we will go.

We'll catch a fox

And put him in a box

And never let him go!'

Lady Sniper joined in, drumming her hands on the table.

Oh a-hunting we will go.

A-hunting we will go.

We'll pot a moose

And decorate the hoose

And never let him go!'

The Colonel took the lid of the breakfast dish and began to bang on it with a spoon.

Oh a-hunting we will go.

A-hunting we will go.'

Lady Sniper seized the coffee pot and beat upon it with her fork. They marched around the table.

We'll shoot them all

And nail 'em to the wall

And leave them there for show!'

Their voices grew more raucous with every note. In the jungle, birds flew up, screaming harsh, warning cries. Animals trembled and hid. Inside the house, a hundred silent heads watched them with two hundred glassy eyes.

The Snipers finished their parade along the veranda and dropped back into their chairs.

'Oh, Johnny!' Lady Sniper cried. 'What fun!'

She looked out at the Thickening Jungle, full of so many kinds of animal just waiting to be blasted to bits. You could shoot a different one every day and not get bored. She smiled at her husband.

'Life is wonderful,' she said.

Chapter Four

'How terrible!' I cried, appalled.

'It was worse than terrible,' said Daphne. 'Wicked, that's what it was. None of us was safe. The whole jungle was living in fear. Every day they were out hunting. Bang! Bang! You couldn't hear yourself think. And if they didn't get you, there was still that dog to watch out for.'

'Yes, Wattles. Ugly great thing, wasn't he, Daphne?'

'Vicious.'

'He started it all really, didn't he?'

'Please,' I said hastily. 'Don't miss anything out. If the dog was important, I must know.'

The crocodiles talked quietly together for a moment, muttering and grunting while I sat patiently, the forest dappling darkness over my pale, white legs.

Then at last they spoke: Harry, then Daphne, then Harry again, each taking up the story in turn so that nothing should be missed.

It was Harry's custom of an evening to swim up-river.

'Off for a bit of warthog with the lads,' as he put it.

Daphne growled.

One night, he returned late and settled himself in the mud next to Daphne, who was pretending to be asleep. He belched quietly.

'Heartburn,' he said, and tried to rub his chest. He belched again, more loudly. Creatures in the trees overhanging the Heavy River woke up and peered down nervously. Daphne opened one eye.

'Heartburn,' Harry said again, grinning sheepishly. 'Terrible it is, love.'

Daphne was unimpressed.

'You'll get no sympathy from me,' she said. 'I've told you before about eating things before they've had a chance to decompose properly. And what time do you call this to be coming back, waking everybody up?'

'At least I wasn't singing,' said Harry. 'Anyway, what have I missed? … Nothing.'

Daphne turned a cold eye on him.

'The Snipers,' she said. 'If that's nothing.'

Harry groaned in the darkness.

'Go on,' he said. 'Who did they get this time? Was it that old jaguar? I've warned him before about them, but he's half daft now …'

Daphne cut across him impatiently.

'No, not him,' she said crossly.
'Actually, it wasn't the Snipers
themselves this time. It was that dog. It
managed to get right down here
without any warning. You remember
that family of gibbons, over there in the
big tree, four little ones? He had the
lot.' She shifted unhappily in the water.
'Didn't eat them neither.'

Harry gave a whistle of disgust.

I had to interrupt.

'But surely,' I said, 'pardon my saying
so, but you kill other animals, don't
you? Isn't that the Law of the Jungle?'

'It is not,' said Daphne firmly.

'Not at all,' said Harry. 'Kill for food,
yes. Kill for fun, never.'

'You kill it, you eat it,' said Daphne.

'Even if it gives you heartburn,' said Harry.

They fixed me with a very serious stare.

'I apologize,' I said. 'I did not fully understand. I see now. I had not meant to interrupt. Please carry on.'

The jungle was in uproar. The poor

gibbons had set up a terrible wailing.
The birds had called out in anger. The
monkeys had chattered their fury from
the high trees. In the river, Daphne
lashed the water to a boiling frenzy with
her tail.

'Something,' everyone had agreed,
'should be done.'

No one knew what.

Harry fell silent, the pain in his chest
forgotten, and when dawn came, the
life of the Thickening Jungle went on
its steady, beating way.

A few nights later, Harry came home
late again. He slid superbly into his
place beside Daphne, only this time he
landed a smacking kiss on the side of
her head.

'Lay off, Harry,' she said crossly.

'You're breath's horrible. What have you been eating now? You smell disgusting. And you've got indigestion again, haven't you? I can always tell.'

Harry winced as his great belly rumbled. He tried to turn it into a grin.

'You see,' scolded Daphne. 'Look at you. What was it this time? Warthog? Okapi? Jungle pig? I don't know which is worse.'

A great belch rose in Harry's throat. He opened his jaws wide and the sound echoed into the night, startling the sleeping jungle. Satisfied, he snuggled further into the mud and closed his eyes.

'None of them,' he said smugly. 'This time I had that dog.'

Chapter Five

'You what?!' cried Daphne, swinging her great head round in alarm. 'You ate Wattles?'

'I did,' said Harry. 'Lock, stock and spiky collar.'

He fought down another rumble, gave up, opened his mouth and ejected a ragged strip of leather, studded with metal. A single tag hung

from the buckle. It said 'WATTLES'.

'Oh, Harry, say it isn't true,' wailed
Daphne, who could not read, of course.

Harry began to look uncomfortable,
only this time it wasn't indigestion.

'It is true, Daphne,' he said. 'Honest.
I thought you'd be pleased. You said
something ought to be done about him.
Good riddance, I say. And at least I ate

him too. You know the rules, the Law of the Jungle.'

'Don't talk to me about the Law of the Jungle,' said Daphne, snorting with agitation. 'And just because you ate him, it doesn't make it all right. You weren't really hungry, were you? That was revenge, that was. But that's not the point. When the Snipers find out you ate their dog, they'll be after you.'

'How will they know it was me?' said Harry. 'I didn't exactly leave a visiting card.'

'I don't know,' said Daphne unhappily. 'But they're human, aren't they? They're clever. They have a way of finding things out. What did happen, anyway? You'll have to tell me or I'll never settle.'

'It was easy,' said Harry. 'Too easy. I'd

swum down to the bend opposite the house, and I was lying low under that overhanging bank. I could see the house from there. The Snipers were inside. I could hear them singing and laughing. It gave me earache. They were fixing another trophy on their wall, as if they don't have enough already. All those stuffed heads, those glass eyes. They give me the willies. I couldn't quite see, but I think it was that jaguar.'

'Poor old thing,' said Daphne.

'He had it coming to him,' said Harry. 'He was getting daft. Anyway, then the woman says, "Lovely, darling, now how about a little drinky-pooh?" You know how she carries on. "Just the ticket," says the Colonel, and out they come on to the veranda, only *now* they've got the dog with them. Then they mix themselves the drinks and settle down.

'After a while, just as I'd hoped, the dog gets bored. It gets up and starts to waddle across the lawn. "Come on, you old darling," I say under my breath, and I let myself drift across the river, nice and slow.

'I can hear it getting closer. I brace my hind legs in the mud, and push myself up so I'm just level with the

bank, but still hidden. Now I can see him, sniffing around, slobbering away. So I make a little noise, not much, but it works. Over he comes, snuffle, snuffle, and …'

Harry opened his massive jaws and closed them with a snap.

'I got him.'

Daphne let out her breath in a long sigh.

'So the Snipers didn't see anything,' she said. 'Thank goodness!'

Harry said nothing.

'Harry?' said Daphne sharply. 'They didn't see, did they?'

Harry shifted a little.

'Well,' he said, avoiding her eye, 'they must have noticed something, because I heard them shouting. But I was well away by then.'

Daphne closed her eyes and groaned.

'Oh, Harry,' she said, and she sounded tired. 'They saw all right. Oh, how could you be so stupid? They'll be after you now. You mark my words. They loved that dog.'

Harry snuggled deeper into the mud.

'Now don't you go worrying your head, Daphne,' he said. 'I'll be all right. I'll be careful.'

'You'd better be,' said Daphne. But her heart beat heavy in her chest.

Chapter Six

The trunk of the Trembling Tree was hard against my back. My legs ached with sitting. I rose to my feet and stretched painfully.

'Are you all right?' said Daphne, looking at me sharply.

'Yes, yes,' I assured her. 'Just a trifle stiff.'

'You're probably hungry too,' said

Harry. 'I know I am.'

'You're always hungry,' said Daphne crossly. 'But this poor gentleman's been listening to us rattling on without so much as a drink of water. Haven't you, dear?'

I held up my flask.

'Soon remedied,' I said cheerfully.

The water was warm and tasted of metal.

'What about food?' said Harry. 'How are you fixed?'

I opened my tin of Fortifying and Sustaining Snacks and looked inside.

'What've you got there?' asked Harry. 'Anything good?'

'Not really,' I said, smiling a little wistfully. 'Dry biscuits. Raisins. Melted chocolate.'

Harry made a face.

'Don't you worry,' said Daphne. 'I'll
see you get something decent.'

She lifted her head and gave a
strange call, like a strangled bark,
ending in a cough. Her breath drifted
across the water, making me stagger
and clutch at the tree. It was very, very
strong.

Gibbons chattered and cried in the

branches above me. I could hear them swinging away into the jungle.

'Won't be a tick now,' said Daphne.

I sat down again and waited curiously, maybe only a few minutes, maybe hours; time had changed so much for me since I entered the jungle. At last there was a movement in the tree above me. I looked up.

Several small, brown, wrinkled faces were peering at me through the branches. Catching my eye, they squealed and disappeared amongst the leaves, but as they did so, a shower of fruits fell into my lap. I cried out, startled, and heard Harry laughing.

'There you are,' said Daphne. 'Something that's fresh.'

I looked at the fruits in my lap. There were soft ruby globes, smooth and glossy; hairy green clusters with snake-patterned skin; fat purple and yellow orbs, bursting from their rinds. I had never seen such riches.

'Are they safe to eat?' I asked, suddenly cautious.

'Of course,' said Daphne. 'The apes love them and you're a kind of ape, aren't you?'

Her comment surprised me. I looked away, embarrassed.

'Yes,' I said. 'I suppose I am.'

My cheeks burned red as mangoes.

'There you are then,' said Daphne comfortably. 'Eat up. They'll do you good.'

Moisture clung stickily to my hands and chin, and dribbled down my rumpled shirt. I had never before tasted such exotic fruits. O Nature! What gifts you offer to comfort the weary, and sustain the Seeker after Truth.

When I was done, I washed my face and hands with water from the river and took my place again at the Trembling Tree.

'Thank you for your patience, dear crocodiles,' I said. 'And for that exquisite feast.'

Here, Daphne giggled.

'Excellent reptiles,' I said, 'do continue. But unless my eyes deceive me, you did indeed escape the Snipers and their guns, Harry.'

'Ah,' said Harry. 'You would think that, wouldn't you, looking at me now? But that's where you'd be wrong.'

Chapter Seven

For a few days, all was well. Harry and Daphne lay low, eating food from their underwater larder when they were hungry. They could hear the Snipers roaming the jungle. Their voices were no longer loud with cheerfulness, but angry and terrible. The Thickening Jungle trembled and hid.

But soon life returned to normal.

Harry ventured out again and rediscovered indigestion. Daphne still worried.

Then, one night, Harry did not come back. Daphne woke suddenly in the early dawn and knew she was alone. She lay in the mud and waited as the sun rose in the sky until, at last, she set off up-river, calling Harry's name.

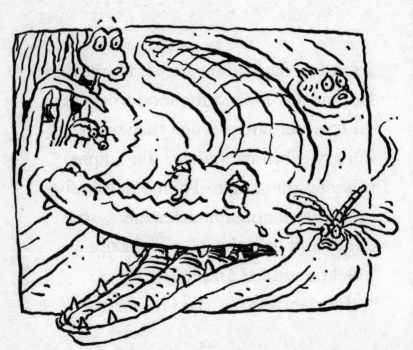

None of the lads had seen him, they said. They'd had a nice fat jungle pig. Not like Harry to miss that. Daphne thanked them sadly and asked them to keep a watch out for him.

For several days she roamed up and down the Heavy River asking for news. No one had seen him. No one could help.

At last she knew she must gather her courage and look in the one place she feared most: the Snipers' house. So, as the sun was setting, she swam slowly down to the overhanging bank where she settled down to watch the house.

It was full of lights. Figures moved about inside. Laughter floated across the lawn to the river.

So, thought Daphne, they aren't angry any more.

She thought it was a bad sign.

The Snipers came out on to the veranda. Lady Sniper was carrying something that dangled from her arm on two thin straps.

'Look, Johnnie!' she cried cheerfully. 'Isn't it divine? At least that old brute was good for something.'

Daphne had to see. Slowly, quietly, she pushed her way across the river and heaved her great bulk on to the end of the Snipers' lawn. Keeping low, she crept into the undergrowth and began to circle towards the house. It was a long way and she was not comfortable on anything other than flat, clear land. Her body was broad and heavy. Her legs were made for gripping or running, not creeping and pushing through thick vegetation.

At last she was nearly at the house.
She stopped and peered through the
thick grass.

The Snipers were inside admiring
their latest trophy. It was, Daphne
noticed sadly, the old jaguar. The thing
Lady Sniper had been waving in the air
was standing on the veranda table.

Even from that distance something about it looked familiar. Daphne strained forward, but still she could not see it properly. She swallowed hard, ignored all her instincts to stay hidden, and ran quickly and quietly across to the veranda.

The object on the table was a large, greeny-brown handbag, square and squat and fastened with an ugly metal clasp. It was made of leather, but not the smooth leather of ox-hides. This was wrinkled and scaled like the hide of a reptile, the hide of a crocodile.

Daphne recognized it at once. Lifting her great head, she wailed her despair to the stars.

'Oh no!' she howled. 'They got my Harry!'

Inside the house the Snipers began to

shout. Daphne heard Colonel Sniper calling for his gun. Quickly she turned and ran. By the time the Snipers burst out on to the veranda, Daphne had slipped into the river and the jungle was quiet once more.

That night, the Heavy River echoed with a distant, bitter sobbing and its muddy waters mingled with a crocodile's tears.

Chapter Eight

Daphne cried all night until by dawn
she lay exhausted in the mud. All hope
was gone. The Snipers had found
Harry, her Harry. They had taken him
and turned him into a handbag. That
once proud hide now held that wicked
woman's knick-knacks. It was wrong.
It was against nature. It was hopeless.

Daphne lay listlessly while the Heavy

River washed her gently with its healing waters until at last she fell into an unhappy doze. She dreamed of Harry.

Waking with a start, she looked round quickly, but there was no one there. The dream had been nothing more than a dream and now even that comfort had fled. It was then that she saw the old gibbon sitting on a rock a little way downstream. It was watching her. As she looked, it beckoned.

Daphne hesitated. Gibbons never, *ever* wanted to meet crocodiles. They would scold you from the trees. The young ones would throw fruit and sticks at you, but that was all.

The gibbon beckoned again. Daphne pushed back into the water and let herself float downstream until she was opposite the rock. There she brought

herself up at a polite distance.

'You called,' she said.

'I did,' said the gibbon.

There was an awkward pause.

'Why?' said Daphne. 'I'm sorry, but
I've got a lot on my mind at the
moment.'

'I know,' said the gibbon. 'That's why I'm here.'

Daphne twitched her tail. Water swirled around her.

'Is it about my Harry?' she said.

'It is,' said the gibbon. 'I might be able to help.'

'How?' said Daphne, sad again. 'It's too late now. He's a handbag. Not even a nice one neither.'

'Ah,' said the gibbon. 'It's a problem, that is. But not beyond hope.'

'You gibbons talk in riddles,' said Daphne. 'I've had a bad night. You're making my head ache.'

'Patience,' said the gibbon.

It settled itself more comfortably on the rock and fluffed out its grizzled fur.

'I am Arthur,' it said importantly. 'The oldest and wisest of the gibbons.'

Daphne had doubts as to how wise even the wisest gibbon could be, but she said nothing.

'We gibbons know your Harry ate that dog, Wattles, for us. We feel we owe him something.'

'That's very nice of you,' said Daphne, touched. 'But you're a bit late now.'

'Not necessarily,' said Arthur. 'I have a plan. We gibbons get about, and I, as the oldest and wisest, have been about more than most. In my travels I have seen many strange and wonderful things, but none stranger than the man who lives up a tree.'

'The what?' said Daphne.

The gibbon looked at her severely.

'Over there.' He waved a paw towards the heart of the jungle. 'He lives in a tree in a clearing. He is a wise and holy man.'

'How do you know?' said Daphne.

'Because he told me so,' said Arthur with dignity. 'He contemplates the Meaning of Life. He studies the Universe.'

'What's the universe?' said Daphne.

Arthur became suddenly angry.

'I don't know!' he shouted. 'I don't know everything, do I? But I'm sure he does. Look, do you want me to help you or not?'

'I'm sorry, Arthur,' said Daphne quickly. 'Of course I do. It's just the thought of humans makes me nervous.'

'This one's all right,' said Arthur. 'He wouldn't hurt a fly. It's his religion. Whatever that is. We've become quite friendly over the years.'

'That's nice for both of you, I'm sure,' said Daphne. 'But I still don't see how he can help. Sitting on your own up a tree thinking about the meaning of life is all very well, but can he *do* anything?'

'Ah,' said Arthur, tapping his stubby nose. 'Here's the interesting part. Before he became a Seeker after Truth he used

to practise the magic arts. For healing purposes, he said. He won't have anything to do with it now, but he still has a few things: potions, powders. He showed me some once.'

'Do you really think he might help?' said Daphne, new hope blossoming in her breast.

'What have you got to lose?' said Arthur.

Daphne raised herself up in the water.

'Lead me to him,' she said.

'It's a long way,' said the gibbon, 'for a crocodile. We can only go so far along the river, but then it's cross-country. Do you think you can manage it?'

Daphne flexed her great shoulders. A flinty light sparked in her eyes.

'I'll just have to,' she said.

Chapter Nine

It was a long way. Poor Daphne found herself wondering whether she would ever make it. At first she had swum steadily up-river while Arthur swung through the trees along the bank, but then they had left the waters of the Heavy River and set their course for the heart of the Thickening Jungle. Daphne struggled through the heavy vegetation. Arthur had tried coaxing, then scolding. Neither worked. At last he accepted she could go no faster and settled down to ride on her back. There he sat, picking his fleas and calling out directions.

Daphne was beginning to flag. She was sure she could hardly take another step, her legs ached so much, when she felt Arthur jump off her back.

'Here we are,' he said. 'Through those creepers ahead.'

It took all Daphne's strength to push her way through the dense vines. On the other side, she found herself in a small, grassy clearing, in the middle of which stood a mighty Trembling Tree.

She sank to the ground with a sigh.

'Ooh!' she said. 'Let me take the weight off my legs.'

'I'll go and look for the man,' said
Arthur. 'He's probably meditating.'

He scampered across to the tree and
disappeared into the branches. Daphne
waited. She could see the leaves moving
as he climbed. Then they stopped.

'Hello, Arthur,' said a quiet voice
from inside the tree.

The hermit was small, thin and balding.
He had climbed down from the tree
and was standing, looking at Daphne.
He wore a single coil of vine around his
middle, which dangled almost to his
toes. Daphne thought it looked rather
attractive. Arthur sat on the ground
beside him, trying to look wise.

'So,' said the hermit, 'what can I do
for you? You do realize,' he added, 'that
I was close, at last, to understanding

everything. Then Arthur disturbed me. I
hope you have a good reason.'

He didn't look as cross as he sounded.
Daphne decided understanding
everything couldn't be so special after
all.

'Oh, I have,' she said earnestly. 'It's
about Harry. The Snipers got my Harry

and turned him into a handbag. I want him back.'

The hermit gave her a kindly look.

'Harry was your friend, wasn't he?' he said gently.

'Oh, he was!' cried Daphne. 'The best friend a girl could have. I mean, he was a bit of a rough diamond. Coming home all hours. Giving himself indigestion. But he was kind and funny and he wouldn't hurt anything unless he had to. And now he's gone!'

She opened her massive jaws and let out a howl of dismay. Her breath gusted over the hermit, who quickly stepped back and put his hand over his face.

'A handbag!' wailed Daphne. 'A rotten little handbag!'

She began to cry again.

'There, there,' said the hermit. 'Not to worry. I think I have just the thing for you. Wait here.'

'I couldn't move if I tried,' muttered Daphne.

The hermit returned from the tree almost immediately, carrying a small pouch on a string. Daphne watched him warily.

'This is Reversing Powder,' he said proudly. 'It's a recipe of my own. It works rather well. Watch.'

He opened his hand to reveal a scrap of cloth.

'This is cotton,' he said, 'from the time when I used to wear clothes.'

He squatted down and put it on the ground. Then he took a pinch of powder from the pouch and sprinkled it on top.

Nothing happened.

Daphne opened her mouth.

'Wait,' said the hermit.

Suddenly the cloth began to move. It lifted a little and twisted on itself. Now it was a heap of separate threads.

'Oooh!' breathed Daphne, but the hermit held up his hand.

The cloth was still changing.

Now it was a fluffy ball of raw cotton. Now it put out little green shoots and, in an instant, a single cotton plant was growing in the ground in front of Daphne's nose.

'You must be careful not to use too much,' said the hermit. 'You want your Harry back, not the egg he hatched from.'

He smiled.

'Here,' he said. 'Good luck. And don't come back if you can help it. There's a dear.'

He knelt and hung the pouch round Daphne's neck.

'Remember,' he said. 'Just a pinch.'

The last Daphne ever saw of him was his skinny legs disappearing up into the leafy branches of the Trembling Tree.

Chapter Ten

I sprang up, scattering fruit rinds.

'Tell me!' I cried. 'Where is this holy recluse? I will seek him out! He must show me too the path to understanding!'

Harry and Daphne exchanged glances.

'Probably still up his tree,' said Daphne. 'If he hasn't already found absolute truth and been reabsorbed into the cosmos.'

'Been what?' said Harry.

'Reabsorbed into the cosmos,' said Daphne patiently. 'That's what Arthur said he wanted, but don't ask me what it means.'

'Please!' I cried. 'Dear Daphne, tell me where this tree is to be found.'

'No,' said Daphne. 'I won't. I'm sorry. He was very good to us, that man, but he didn't want to be disturbed. He said so. If you want to understand the meaning of life, you'll just have to find out for yourself.'

I sat down sadly and hung my head. How foolish I had been. How impetuous. The dried and empty rinds lay around me, like fallen jewels in the mud.

'Shall I go on?' said Daphne, not unkindly.

I gestured feebly and nodded.

The journey back to the Heavy River was even harder. Daphne was tired, but she struggled on bravely. At the riverside, she allowed Arthur to take the pouch from her neck and sank down gratefully into the waters. There she let the current carry her down-stream. Arthur followed on the bank to the bend opposite the Snipers', where Daphne heaved herself out of the water. The two animals sat side by side in the undergrowth, staring across at the house.

Dusk was falling. Lights shone from the windows. The Snipers were on the veranda, drinking and laughing. There was no sign of the handbag.

'He … it must be inside,' whispered
Daphne.

'It must be,' agreed Arthur. 'The
problem is, how do we get into the
house without being noticed?'

'Can't you think of something?' said
Daphne.

'Why me?' said Arthur.

'Because you're the oldest and wisest
of the gibbons, that's why.'

Arthur scratched his head.

'Let me think,' he said. 'What we need is a distraction. Wait here.'

'Don't go off with the powder,' said Daphne. 'Put it back round my neck. I'd never forgive myself if anything happened to it.'

'Or to me, I hope,' muttered Arthur as he swung away through the trees.

He was back very quickly.

'It's all fixed,' he said. 'In a few moments there'll be a terrific racket on the other side of the lawn. We have to be ready. Let's get as close to the house as we can.'

In fact, they were almost level with the veranda when the most incredible hooting and squealing broke out in the trees by the river.

Lady Sniper screamed and spilled her drink.

'Johnnie!' she shrieked. 'What is it?'

The Colonel had already seized his gun.

'I don't know,' he growled. 'But I'll soon sort them out. Come on, Caro!'

The two humans set off across the lawn.

'Now!' hissed Arthur. 'Quickly!'

Daphne raised herself on her toes and, breaking cover, ran swiftly across to the veranda. Arthur bounded along at her side. In a twinkling, they were inside the house.

They found themselves in the trophy room. Row upon row of heads stared blankly down from the wall. The old

jaguar gazed blindly at them from beside the fireplace.

'It's awful,' breathed Daphne. 'Just look at them. Poor things.'

'Never mind them,' said Arthur. 'We've got a handbag to find.'

A quick search of the room revealed a wealth of strange items all made from the Snipers' victims. But no handbag.

'We'll have to try upstairs,' said
Arthur. 'Can you manage?'

But Daphne was already clawing her
way up the broad wooden steps.

The handbag was sitting in the middle
of the Snipers' bed. Daphne fumbled
with the pouch.

'Help me, Arthur,' she said. 'I'm all
fingers and no thumbs.'

The gibbon deftly opened the little
pouch and placed a pinch of powder in
his palm.

'Here,' he said. 'You should do this.
Blow.'

Daphne blew. The powder drifted
across the bed and settled on the
handbag. The watching animals held
their breath.

The bag began to swell and bulge. A

snout pushed out on one side. A tail grew from the other. Four legs shot out, one at each corner. There was a heave and a shudder and then there stood Harry, grinning as only a crocodile can.

'Hello, darling,' he said. 'What kept you? And who's your little friend?'

Chapter Eleven

Daphne did not have time to reply as the bed suddenly collapsed with a crash under Harry's enormous weight.

'Oh no,' said Arthur. 'The Snipers will have heard us now. We'd better scarper.'

But Daphne stopped him.

'Look,' she said. 'Some of the powder must have fallen on to the bed.'

The cotton sheets were writhing and twitching, just as the hermit's scrap of cloth had done. The wooden bedposts were twisting and gnarling and putting out green shoots. The woollen bedspread humped itself into a ball, grew ears, a tail and a pair of horns, and a large, startled sheep bolted past them for the stairs.

'Blimey!' said Harry. 'What is that stuff?'

'Reversing Powder,' said Daphne. 'It changes things back to what they were before.'

'Right,' said Harry briskly. 'Is there any left?'

'Quite a lot,' said Arthur.

'Good,' said Harry. 'Let's do the house. Time to introduce Colonel and Lady Sniper to some of their victims.'

The three animals charged through the house. Arthur carried the pouch, scattering Reversing Powder right and left. Behind them everything was exploding into life.

Hearing the noise, the Snipers had raced back to the veranda. They stood in the doorway struck dumb with horror at what they saw. Two great crocodiles were thrashing through the house, beating their massive tails about them. Above them, leaping from cupboard to mantelpiece to chair, was an old, grizzled gibbon, clutching a pouch in its paws and scattering clouds of dust in the air. Down the stairs tumbled an avalanche of wildlife.

Peacock fans fluttered, screamed and spread their tails. Snakeskin belts slithered and writhed along the sprouting wooden banisters. A pigskin case ran squealing between the Snipers' legs and disappeared into the forest.

The Colonel tried to raise his gun, but as he did so, Lady Sniper's ivory hairbrush joined forces with the elephant-foot umbrella stand and a huge, enraged bull elephant exploded out of the hallway flapping its ears and trumpeting.

The Snipers turned and fled. The Colonel was fast, but not fast enough. He was barely halfway across the lawn when, with a mighty leap, the tiger-skin rug brought him down. A cheer went up from all sides.

'Look!' cried Daphne. 'Lady Sniper's getting away!'

The Colonel's lady had put on a tremendous burst of speed and, in spite of the bravest efforts of the old jaguar, was leaving her pursuers well behind.

'Don't let her get to the jeep!' cried Daphne, but Lady Sniper had already thrown herself into the driver's seat and was fumbling with the keys.

'Harry! Do something!' Daphne cried in despair.

Harry was clutching his chest and wincing.

'Oh never mind your heartburn now,' Daphne wailed.

Harry rose magnificently to the occasion. With one almighty belch, he ejected a lipstick, a powder compact, a set of keys, a handkerchief, a packet of hairpins and a handful of loose change.

Then he plunged from the creaking, rocking house and made for the river.

'I'll head her off at the ford,' he shouted.

Then, with an almighty splash, he was gone.

Daphne and Arthur stood on the lawn, watching the animals and birds disappearing back into the jungle. Of the Snipers' house there was now no sign, other than a dense thicket of Trembling Trees in the middle of a grassy clearing.

Daphne looked at Arthur.

'He will get her, won't he?' she said.

'Bound to,' said Arthur. 'Fine big crocodile like that.'

They were silent for a while.

'You know what,' said Daphne at last.

'You don't look like the oldest and wisest of the gibbons any more.'

'What do you mean?' said Arthur indignantly.

'That powder. You must have got some on yourself. All your wrinkles have gone.'

It was dark when Harry came home. He slid quietly in beside Daphne and settled himself in the mud.

'Is that you?' she whispered.

'Of course it is. Who else would it be?'

Daphne sighed.

'I've missed you,' she said. 'I can't begin to tell you how much.'

She nuzzled him with her snout. Something rumbled deep in Harry's chest.

'Indigestion,' he said cheerfully.

'Did you get her then?' said Daphne. 'I hardly dare ask.'

'Now don't you go fretting about her,' said Harry. 'She won't be bothering anyone any more.'

'Promise?'

'Promise.'

He opened his mighty jaws and the

belch he uttered sounded triumphantly through the Thickening Jungle. A pair of glasses flew from his gaping throat and landed on the river bank where they lay winking in the moonlight. After a moment, they turned quietly into a small, puzzled tortoise, which crept softly away into the reeds.

Chapter Twelve

For a long time, no one spoke. The crocodiles lay quietly in the river, watching, waiting.

I tried to collect my thoughts. At last I found a few feeble words.

'It seems so incredible,' I said.

'It's the way it was,' said Daphne. 'Every word is true.'

'But how shall I make my report?' I

said. 'It's impossible.'

'Not our problem,' said Harry cheerfully. 'Now, if you'll excuse us …'

He nudged Daphne and winked, definitely winked.

I stood and held my safari hat.

'Goodbye,' said Daphne. 'It's been ever so nice talking to you.'

I bowed, deeply moved.

'Thank you, dear lady,' I said. 'It has been an honour and a pleasure.'

'Ta-ta, mate,' said Harry. 'And good luck.'

'Goodbye, Harry,' I said. 'Take care of yourself, and of Daphne.'

They were sinking into the river now. The water swirled sluggishly around them. Tears pricked my eyes.

I could hear their voices as they swam up-river, two knobbled shapes barely breaking the surface.

'Wasn't he lovely, Harry? Such beautiful manners.'

'Oh yes, Daph. He was a real gent.'

'Do you think he'll be back?'

'No. What for?'

'It's a shame really.'

'Cheer up, old girl, and give us a kiss.

There we are. And a smile. Lovely. You see, life goes on.'

'Oh it does, Harry. It does indeed.'

Epilogue

The next day, I left the Thickening
Jungle and returned to my office,
although now it seemed cramped and
stuffy. I wrote in my report that the
Snipers had disappeared without trace,
which was no more nor less than the
truth, as Harry and Daphne told me.
The incident was filed as another
unexplained mystery and forgotten.

Now I am leaving the consulate, retiring after forty-two years of loyal service. But I shall not return to England. The Thickening Jungle calls me back.

Tonight I shall return to it, taking nothing, leaving everything, including this, my last report. There, I shall cast my clothes into the Heavy River and wrap myself in creepers. I shall drink the dew in the morning and eat the fruits the animals bring me.

And there will be no more words.